LYNN REISER

MARGARET AND MARGARITA

MARGARITA Y MARGARET

GREENWILLOW BOOKS NEW YORK

Watercolor paints and a black pen were used for the full-color art.
The text type is Helvetica Black.
Copyright © 1993 by Lynn Whisnant Reiser

Printed in Hong Kong by South China Printing Company (1988) Ltd.
First Edition   10 9 8 7 6 5 4 3 2 1

Library of Congress Cataloging-in-Publication Data
Reiser, Lynn.
Margaret and Margarita, Margarita y Margaret / by Lynn Reiser.
p.   cm.
Summary: Margaret, who only speaks English, and Margarita,
who only speaks Spanish, meet in the park and have fun
playing together even though they have different languages.
ISBN 0-688-12239-6 (trade).   ISBN 0-688-12240-X (lib. bdg.)
[1. Friendship—Fiction.   2. Parks—Fiction.   3. Play—Fiction.
4. Spanish language materials—Bilingual.]   I. Title.
PZ73.R4   1993   [E]—dc20   92-29012   CIP   AC

TO MY FRIENDS AND MIS AMIGAS – SUSAN SUZY BETTIE JANE LORRAINE CLARA RUTH ROSANN ESTHER BETSY INGRID BARBARA SYLVIA ZELDA LOTTIE BRANKA SUSIE ALISON GAIL HARRIET JESSICA ALEX LUCILLE LAURA ISABEL HISAKO PHYLLIS AVA SUSAN

2-28-00 Ingram C (593) 14.34

What a beautiful day

to go to the park,

Margaret.

Qué día más bonito

para ir al parque,

Margarita.

NO.

It is NOT a beautiful day.

I do not want

to go to the park.

And Susan,

my little rabbit,

does not want

to go to the park.

There is no one

to play with.

NO.

NO es un día bonito.

No quiero

ir al parque.

Y Susana,

mi gatita,

no quiere

ir al parque.

No hay nadie

con quien jugar.

Look, Margaret.

There is a little girl and her mother.

Hello.

Oh dear,

they do not speak English.

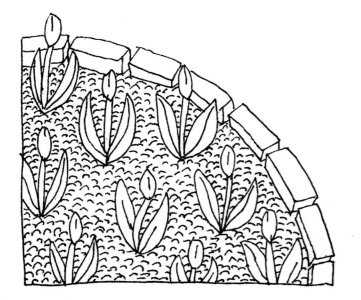

Mira, Margarita.

Allí está una niña con su madre.

Hola.

Oh no,

no hablan español.

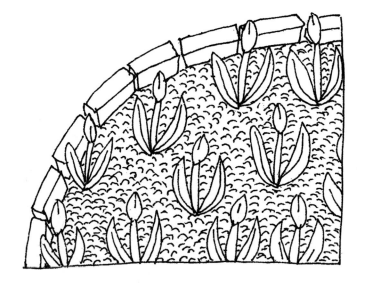

Hello.

Hola.

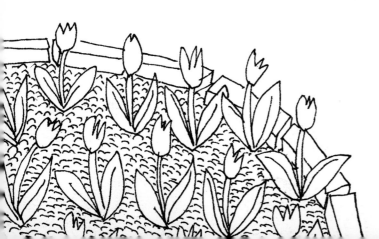

My name is
Margaret.
My rabbit's
name is
Susan.
Susan says,
Hola.

Me llamo
Margarita.
Mi gatita
se llama
Susana.
Susana dice,
Hello.

I like
your purple cat.

I like
your yellow shoes.

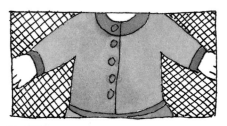

I like
your blue dress.

I like
your green ribbon.

Me gusta
tu conejita amarilla.

Me gustan
tus zapatos marrones.

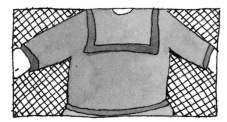

Me gusta
tu vestido verde.

Me gusta
tu cinta morada.

**I like
your red smile.**

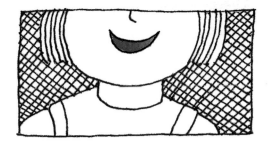

**Me gusta
tu sonrisa colorada.**

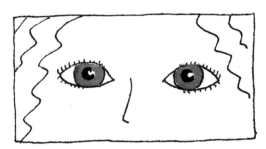

**And I like
your brown eyes.**

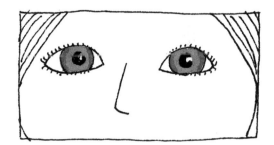

**Y me gustan
tus ojos azules.**

**I like you.
Susan likes you.
Will you be my friend?**

**Tu me gustas.
Tu le gustas a Susana.
¿Te gustaría ser mi amiga?**

Yes!

¡Amigas!

And Susan says,

Yes—¡amigas!

¡Sí!
Friends!
Y Susana dice,
¡Sí!—friends!

This is a beautiful day.

Let's have a party!

¡Qué día más bonito!

¡Hagamos una fiesta!

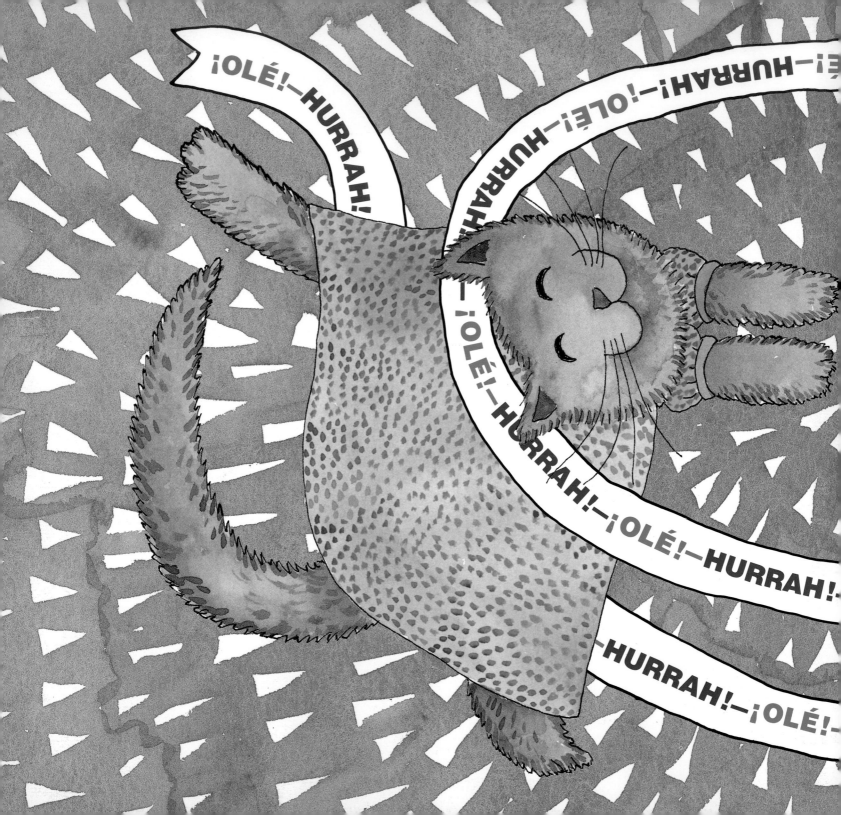

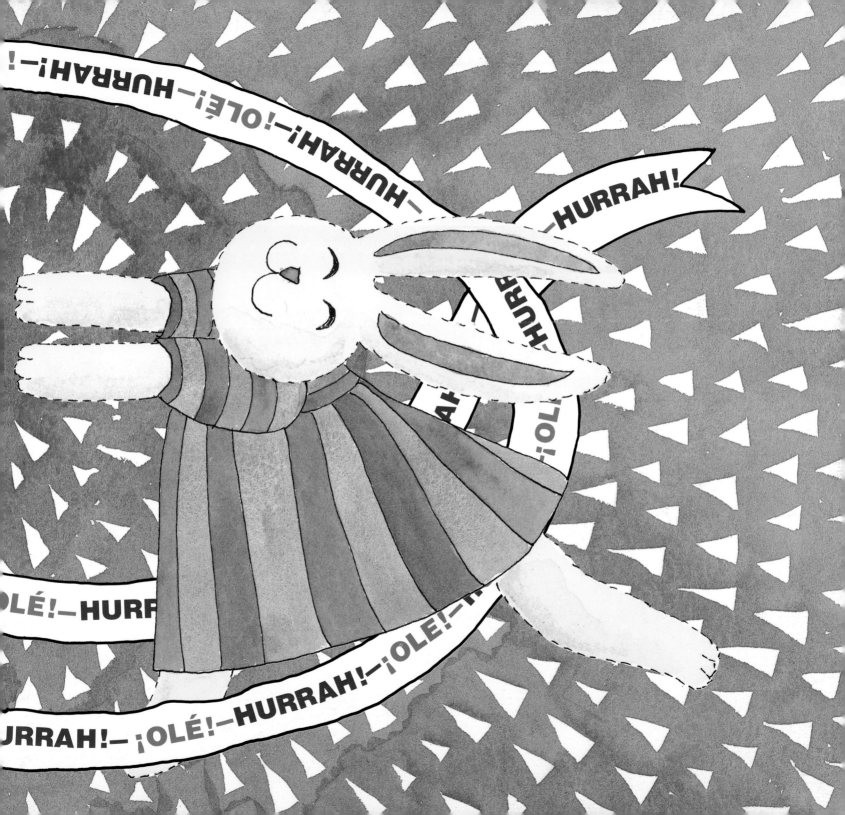

Now let's take a nap.

SWEET DREAMS—QUE SUEÑEN CON LOS ANGELITOS—SWEET

Vamos a hacer la siesta.

REAMS—QUE SUEÑEN CON LOS ANGELITOS— SWEET DREAMS—

Margaret,
it is time
to go home.

**Margarita,
es hora
de volver a casa.**

Margarita,

this is my mother.

Mama,

this is my amiga,

Margarita,

and her gatita,

Susana.

We had

a fiesta

and a siesta.

Margaret,
esta es mi madre.
Mamá,
esta es mi friend,
Margaret,
y su little rabbit,
Susan.
Hicimos
un party
y un nap.

I am happy to meet you,
Margarita and Susana
and Margarita's mother.

Mucho gusto
en conocerles,
Margaret y Susan
y la madre de Margaret.

See you tomorrow,
friends!

¡Hasta mañana,
amigas!

Tomorrow will be a VERY beautiful day to go to the park, Mama!

Adiós, amigas.

Good-bye, friends.

Adiós, friends.

Good-bye, amigas.

Adiós.

Good-bye.

Amigas.

Friends.